Copyright © 1990 by Nord-Süd Verlag AG, Gossau Zürich, Switzerland
First published in Switzerland under the title *Zottels Hundeleben*
English translation copyright © 1990 by Nord-Süd Verlag AG, Gossau Zürich, Switzerland

First published in the United States, Great Britain, Canada,
Australia and New Zealand in 1990 by North-South Books,
an imprint of Nord-Süd Verlag AG, 8625 Gossau Zürich, Switzerland.

Library of Congress Catalog Card Number: 89-43725
ISBN 1-55858-096-4

British Library Cataloguing in Publication Data is available.

1   3   5   7   9   10   8   6   4   2

Printed in Belgium

SHAGGY

By Marcus Pfister

Translated by Lenny Hort

North-South Books
New York

Shaggy lived by himself in the junkyard. He was free to do whatever he wanted all day, and at night he could stretch out comfortably on the back seat of an old car. He never had to worry about a leash tugging at his throat. There was only one problem...

The rats. They came at night and ruined his sleep and stole his food. No matter how fiercely he barked he couldn't scare them away. Some nights there were so many rats that Shaggy just covered his eyes and tried to pretend they weren't there.

One day a cat turned up at the junkyard. "Let me move in with you," she meowed. "I'll get rid of your rats in no time."

"I don't need your help!" the dog growled back at her. The last thing Shaggy wanted was to share his home— especially with a cat.

It wasn't fair. That cat could catch a rat or a mouse any time she was hungry. But Shaggy could stare at a mousehole for hours and never catch a single one.

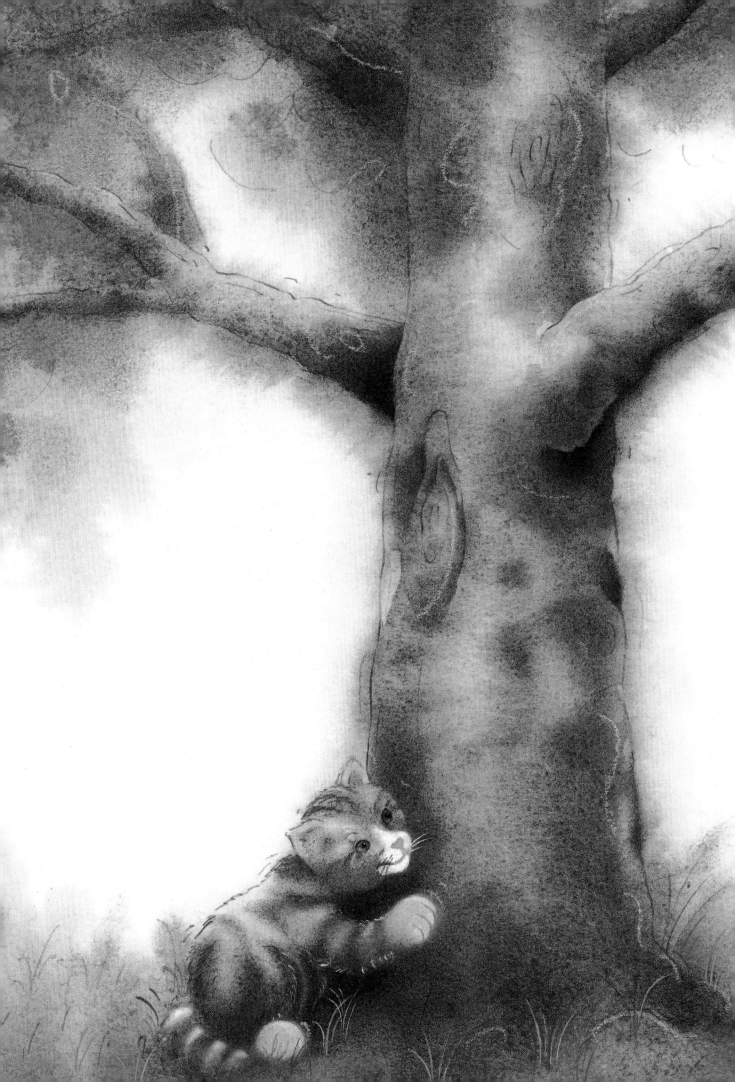

And the cat was great at climbing trees. When
Shaggy tried it he almost broke his neck.

Poor Shaggy had just one thing going for him—his nose. He could sniff out a chunk of meat half a mile away or find a bone buried deep in the ground. So Shaggy pretended to ignore the cat and the rats and went on fending for himself.

Then one day Shaggy's nose led him into a supermarket . . . and out again trailing a string of juicy sausages. The butcher went chasing after him, but Shaggy raced away down the street.

Soon a Great Dane and a boxer joined the chase,
then more and more dogs, all of them bigger and fiercer
than Shaggy. The hungry pack finally caught up—

But while they were busy yapping at each other over all that meat, Shaggy escaped with half a dozen sausages. He was so happy to make it back to the junkyard that he went straight to sleep, dreaming of his tasty prize.

But when Shaggy woke up the sausages were gone. The rats must have taken them! Shaggy finally swallowed his pride and asked the cat for help. "You can move into the back seat with me," he told her.

"Of course I'll help you," said the cat. "What are friends for?"

Then the dog and the cat had the feast of their lives and curled up together in the moonlight.

"I'm glad I'm not all by myself anymore," said Shaggy. But the cat was already asleep.

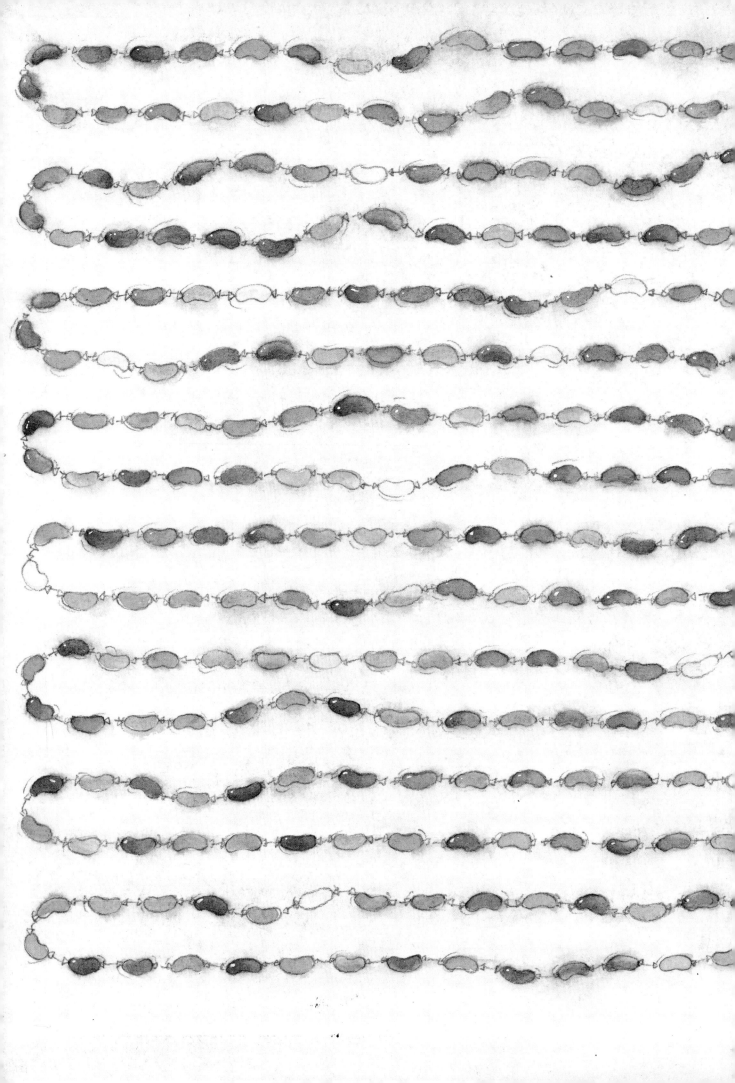